For Iris and Eloi, who take delight in school.
Dany Aubert

For my little ones: Edgar, Arwen, and Violette.
Eve Tharlet

minedition

English edition published 2020 by Michael Neugebauer Publishing Ltd. Hong Kong

Text copyright © 2020 Dany Albert / Catherine Leblanc
Illustrations copyright © 2020 Eve Tharlet
Coproduction with Michael Neugebauer Publishing Ltd., Hong Kong.
Rights arranged with "minedition" Rights and Licensing AG, Zurich, Switzerland.

Michael Neugebauer Publishing Ltd.
Unit 28, 5/F, Metro Centre II, 21 Lam Hing Street, Kowloon Bay, Hong Kong.
Phone +852 2807 1711, e-mail: info@mineditiuon.com
Printed in November 2019 at L.Rex Printing Co. Ltd.
3/F, Blue Box Factory Building, 25 Hing Wo Street, Tin Wan, Aberdeen, Hong Kong, China.
Typesetting in Sabon
Library of Congress Cataloging-in-Publication Data available upon request.

ISBN 978-988-8342-04-4
10 9 8 7 6 5 4 3 2 1
First Impression

For more information please visit our website: www.minedition.com

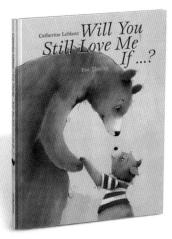

Will You Still Love Me If...?
ISBN 978-988-8240-51-7

Here She Is!
ISBN 978-988-8240-92-0

Too Big Or Too Small?
ISBN 978-988-8341-42-9

Dany Aubert
Catherine Leblanc

School is coming

Pictures by **Eve Tharlet**

minedition

It was bedtime for Martin and his sister Anna.

"Mom," Martin asked, "can you read me another story? Please...? Just one more?"

"It's time to go to sleep now," Mom replied, "but soon it'll be time to start school, and your teacher will read you lots of beautiful stories."

"Oh," Anna exclaimed, "I want a teacher to read me stories, too!"

Martin turned up his little nose and shook his head: "Not me! I don't want to go to school."

The next day Martin woke up full of questions. "Mom, why does my sweater feel so small? And why do I always have to brush my teeth at night?"

"Oh, my little one," Mom said, "think of how many questions you'll be able to ask when you're in school!"

Martin didn't want to hear it. "You're so soft and cozy, Mom," he said, "I want to stay home with you forever."

Martin loved to ride his bike in between Mom and Dad.

"Tomorrow we will ride past your school," Mom said. "You'll like it once you see it."

"No, I certainly won't!" Martin replied, stopping his bike. "I'd rather climb trees with my friends instead."

"Good idea," she said. "We can all climb trees together once we return."

"Can I go to school, too?" Anna asked.

"You're still too young," Mom said. "This year it's Martin's turn."

"He's so lucky!" Anna said.

Later Martin dawdled into the kitchen, his chin quivering.

"My teddy bear feels sad," Martin said. "He doesn't want to go to school…"

"I understand," Mom replied. "He's scared because he's never been to a new place like that before. But you know what? He's still too young to go to school. He will stay at home."

Martin thought he was still too young to go to school, too.

"Would you like to play a guessing game?" Martin's Mom asked.

"Oh, yes!"

"If I wasn't waiting for you after kindergarten, what would you do?"

"I would call you," Martin answered.

"Great!... And if my phone wasn't working?"

"Then I would find a helicopter."

"What terrific ideas you have," Mom said. "You're just as smart as the grown-ups!"

"Me too! 'elicoper!" Anna repeated.

"Not this year, Anna," Mom said. "This year it's Martin's turn."

"Oh, he's so lucky!" Anna said.

"Look, Martin," Mom said, "a brand-new backpack. You can pack your favorite book and your snack when you go to school."

Anna looked at it eagerly. "I want a 'packback,' too!" she exclaimed.

"This year it's Martin's turn," Mom said.

"Oh, he's so lucky," Anna said.

Martin didn't feel very lucky. But he did like the backpack...

One morning Martin asked his Dad, "Can I write a word on your back?"

"Sure!" Dad replied.

Martin began forming letters in his father's fur with his finger.

"What's that one?" Martin asked.

"It's a P!"

"And one more…?"

"A!"

"What's that spell?" asked Martin.

"Pa! Excellent job!"

Martin's eyes lit up. He was proud that he knew his alphabet and a few words.

At breakfast Martin smeared honey on a slice of bread all by himself.

"Mom," Martin wondered, "is the school far away?"

"Not at all," Mom replied. "We can go there by foot."

Martin explained all this to his teddy bear: "You are too small to walk to school, Teddy. But I will tell you all about it when I get home."

"Mom," Martin wondered, "is the school very big?"

"It's bigger than our house, but it's just the right size for all your friends to fit inside," Mom said.

"Really? Even my friend Theo? And Lea?"

"Yes!"

"What about Christopher and Camille?"

"Of course!"

Martin smiled with relief.

"And there's a big playground," Dad added, "where you can play games with all your friends."

"Do you think I can play ball there?" Martin asked.

"Of course!"

"Awesome!"

"Oh, he's so lucky," Anna said again.

"And what if I'm not smart enough?" Martin asked.

"You will do your best, and that's what matters," Mom replied.

"And when Anna is old enough, can we go to school together?" Martin asked.

"I'm sure she would like that."

At last Martin was feeling excited about starting school the next day.

"School is for big kids," he said, "like me!"